Penguin Books Ltd, Harmondsworth, Middlesex, England
A Division of Penguin Books USA Inc.
375 Hudson Street, New York, New York 10014
Penguin Books Australia Ltd, Ringwood, Victoria, Australia
Penguin Books Canada Limited, 2801 John Street, Markham, Ontario, Canada L3R 1B4
Penguin Books (N.Z.) Ltd, 182-190 Wairau Road, Auckland 10, New Zealand

First published by The Viking Press 1956
Viking Seafarer Edition published 1974
Published in Picture Puffins 1983
Reprinted 1986

All rights reserved
Published simultaneously in Canada
ISBN 0 14 050 417 6
Library of Congress catalog card number: 56-13707

Manufactured in the United States of America

WILLIAM PÈNE DU BOIS

LION

Puffin Books

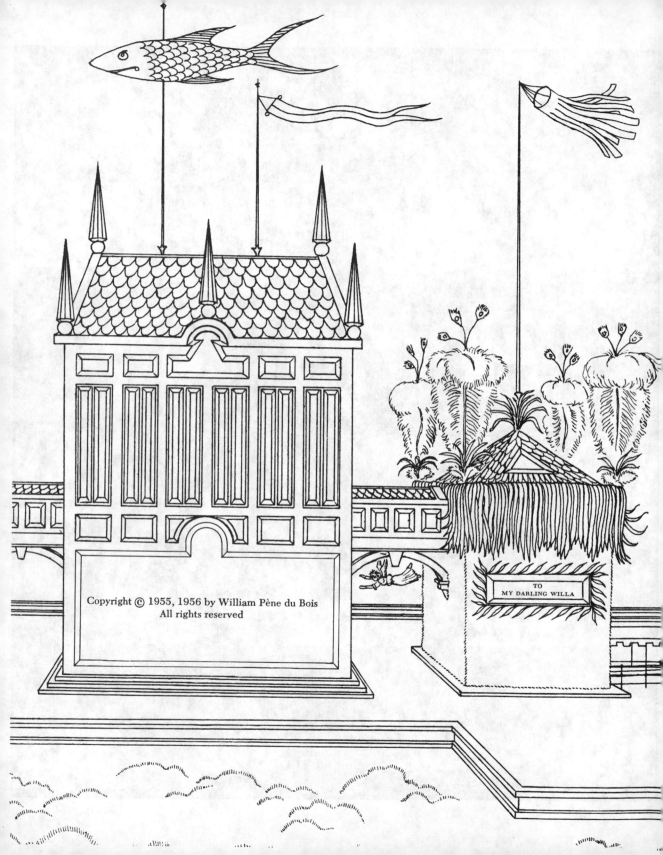

TO
MY DARLING WILLA

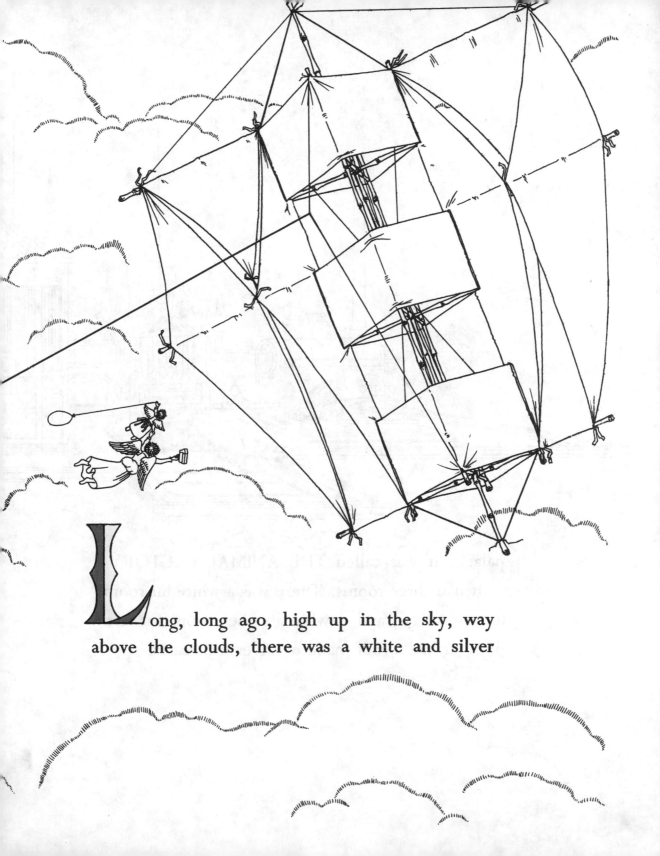

Long, long ago, high up in the sky, way
above the clouds, there was a white and silver

palace. It was called THE ANIMAL FACTORY.
It had three rooms. There was a white fur room
for cold days, and a white feather room for hot
days. It had a roof made of silver fish scales.

High up, just under the roof, there was a bright, light room made of crystal glass and diamond rocks.

It was called THE DRAWING ROOM.

In that room one hundred and four artists sat on silver stools behind one hundred and four white wooden tables. They sat in rows and drew pictures of animals. They worked with sheets of pure white paper, ermine brushes dipped in gold paint, and eight-sided boxes of wax crayons.

They made up new names of animals, which they wrote down in gold letters.

They made up new animals, which they drew in clear colors.

It was in this way that animals were first invented,

      before they were made,

      before they were flown to the Planets of the Universe.

There was one artist who was boss. His name was Foreman.

When he was quite young, Artist Foreman won a medal for the first animal he made up. It was called WORM. Later he grew up and became boss and stopped drawing.

But one day he thought of a new word and the new word was

LION.

"I HAVE MADE UP A WONDERFUL NAME FOR AN ANIMAL!" he shouted.

William Pène du Bois

"I am going to draw an animal and call it LION! It will be BEAUTIFUL!" The other artists were too busy working to hear him.

The other artists made lots of noise while they worked, because they made sounds to go with the animals they drew. THE DRAWING ROOM was filled with MOOS, MEOWS, HOOTS, BOW-WOWS, TWEETS, and WHISTLES.

Artist Foreman went to his closet. He took his drawing table and carried it out into THE DRAW-ING ROOM. He put it near the crystal windows. He reached for his silver stool. He took a sheet of pure white paper, a new ermine brush, his own gold paint, and sharp wax crayons.

He sat down, took his brush, dipped it deep in his own gold paint, and wrote

LION

He wrote it in big letters. He didn't leave much room for his drawing.

"AND NOW I'LL MAKE UP A LION!" he shouted. He looked at his sheet of paper. He scratched his head. He looked some more. He blinked his eyes. After a long time of looking, Artist Foreman said to himself, "It's a funny thing, but I do not quite remember how to make up animals. It's been FOREVER since I made one up! I think I'll look at what the other artists are drawing." He took a walk through the rows of tables.

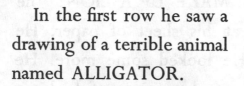

In the first row he saw a
drawing of a terrible animal
named ALLIGATOR.

In the second row he saw
a big furry animal which
looked nicer, named BEAR.

The artist drawing BEAR
was softly growling.

In the third row there was a fat animal with feathers named CHICKEN.

He walked on, looking left and right, until he came to a striped animal named ZEBRA which was in the last row.

"It's beginning to come back to me now," said Artist Foreman. He quickly drew a small, fat animal. He used every one of his colors.

"The LION is good-looking," said Artist Foreman to himself.

He looked at it some more.

He scratched his head and thought, "That is LION, and it will say 'PEEP PEEP.'"

He looked at it some more.

"It's been a long time since I've made up an animal. Maybe the LION isn't quite right, though I'm quite sure that it is." He looked at it some more.

"LION is such a lovely word that maybe I should ask just one other artist for just ONE WORD about LION. Then I'll know that LION is just right."

He took his drawing to an artist in the fourth row and said, "TELL ME IN *ONE WORD* WHAT IS WRONG WITH THE LION."

LION

The artist looked at the SMALL, FAT, BRIGHT animal.

He giggled softly.

He looked up and said,

"SIZE."

Artist Foreman was happy to hear this.

"LION is beautiful," he thought to himself. "LION is so beautiful that it should be much bigger."

He took another sheet of pure white paper. He wrote LION in smaller gold letters. He drew LION much bigger. He said, "PEEP PEEP," as he drew LION.

"Now it is just right," said Artist Foreman.

He looked at it some more.

"I wonder why that artist giggled?"

He looked at it some more.

"Maybe LION still isn't just right," thought Artist Foreman. "I must ask another."

He took his drawing to an artist in the fifth row and said, "TELL ME IN *ONE WORD* WHAT IS WRONG WITH THE LION."

The artist looked at the BIG, FAT, BRIGHT animal.

He giggled softly.

He looked up and said,

"FEATHERS."

Artist Foreman turned red and flew back to his drawing table. NO WONDER the artists were giggling.

Artist Foreman had made a TERRIBLE MIS-TAKE! He had put FEATHERS and FUR on the SAME ANIMAL! He had given LION a crown of feathers around his head and neck.

He looked at it some more.

ARTIST FOREMAN TURNED RED AGAIN!

LION had a tail like a FISH!

"Feathers, fur, and fish scales!"

He quickly took his thumb and pushed it down hard on the drawing of LION. He rubbed all the bright-colored feathers together until they became a YELLOW-BROWN color. He took a DARK-BROWN crayon and covered the head and tail with DARK-BROWN fur. "PEEP PEEP!" he shouted. "Now it is right."

He looked at it some more.

"LION is such a lovely name," he thought. "I must ask another artist about LION." He took his drawing to an artist in the sixth row.

"TELL ME IN *ONE WORD* WHAT IS WRONG WITH THE LION."

The artist looked at the BIG, FAT, BRIGHT, ALL-FUR animal and said,

"COLOR."

Artist Foreman was rather happy to hear this.

It was right for a tiny animal to be all in bright colors, but wrong for a bigger animal.

LION

He took his thumb and pushed it down hard
on the drawing of LION. He rubbed it until the

LION

body and legs were all YELLOW-BROWN.
"PEEP PEEP!" he shouted.

Grasshopper

He looked at it some more.

"The next artist will surely tell me that LION is right," he said to himself. He took the drawing to an artist in the seventh row and said, "TELL ME IN *ONE WORD* WHAT IS WRONG WITH THE LION."

The artist looked quickly at the BIG, FAT, YELLOW-BROWN, ALL-FUR animal and said,

"LEGS."

This made Artist Foreman angry. "I have given LION four legs," he thought. "That's USUALLY right for furry animals!"

He looked at it some more.

"Well, maybe the legs are a little thin for such a fine, fat animal." He made them stronger. "There now, PEEP PEEP!" he said. "I'll ask one more artist, though this time LION is right."

He took the drawing to an artist in the eighth row and said, "TELL ME IN *ONE WORD* WHAT IS WRONG WITH THE LION."

The artist whose turn it was looked at the BIG,
FAT, YELLOW-BROWN, ALL-FUR, STRONG-
LEGGED animal and said,

"HAIRCUT."

Artist Foreman didn't like this at all. He took
the drawing back to his table. He was now VERY
angry! "PEEP PEEP!" he shouted. He looked at
it some more.

"Well, maybe the fur is too shaggy for such a GREAT animal." He took an eraser and rubbed some of it away. He rubbed it off around the body. He rubbed it off around the legs. He rubbed fur off part of the tail. He didn't dare touch the head or the tip of the tail, because he was afraid the feathers and the fish tail might show through.

"LION is now beautiful." He sighed. "*BEAU-TIFUL!*" he shouted. "I am sure LION is right."

He looked at it some more.

"I KNOW LION IS RIGHT, PEEP PEEP!"

He ran with his drawing to an artist in the ninth row and said, "TELL ME IN *ONE WORD* WHAT IS WRONG WITH THE LION."

The artist looked at the BIG, THIN, WELL-TRIMMED, YELLOW-BROWN, ALL-FUR, STRONG-LEGGED animal with the BUSHY MANE and the TASSELED TAIL. He looked at it closely and from far away. He looked at it upside down. He looked at it sideways.

He looked at it through little holes he made with his fists.

He finally looked up at Artist Foreman, smiled, and said,

"NOTHING!"

"AHA!" shouted Artist Foreman, "I KNEW IT!" He tried another artist. "TELL ME IN *ONE WORD* WHAT IS WRONG WITH THE LION."

"NOTHING!"

He tried another artist.

"NOTHING!"

Jumping with joy and laughing and shouting, Artist Foreman hurried off with his drawing to see his boss who was the Chief Designer. He flew through the great windows.

"Yes, Foreman?"

"Oh, Sir," said Artist Foreman, "please, please TELL ME IN *ONE WORD*—I mean, excuse me—I have made up an animal.

William Pène du Bois

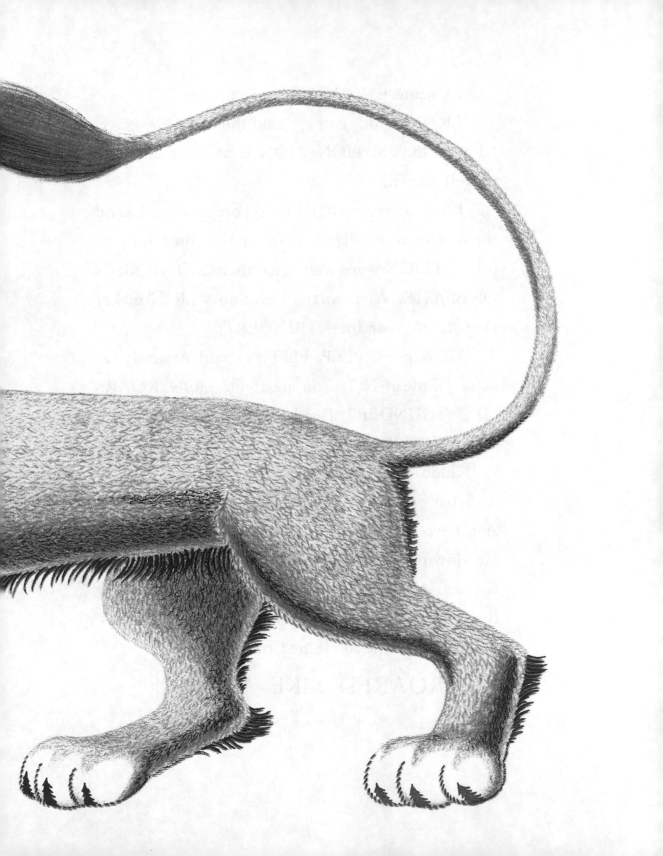

"Its name is *LION*. I bring it to you."

"LION is a nice name," said the Chief Designer. "Let us look at LION. LION is handsome. LION is well drawn.

"I will make two LIONS, Foreman, and send them at once to Planet Earth. I wouldn't be surprised if LION were welcomed there as THE KING OF BEASTS. What sort of noise does LION make? Does LION roar like THUNDER?"

"LION goes 'PEEP PEEP,'" said Artist Foreman. "I mean NO! You are right. LION ROARS LIKE THUNDER! Thank you, Sir. You are too kind, TOO KIND!"

"Good day, Foreman."

Artist Foreman bowed his head, turned quickly, and flew back to THE DRAWING ROOM. He sat down on his silver stool behind his white wooden table. He looked at the heavenly view through the crystal windows. He was feeling VERY HAPPY. He smiled, leaned back, and

ROARED LIKE A LION!